For Nancy and Jack and Commander Master Chief Sagendorf

SIMON & SCHUSTER BOOKS FOR YOUNG READERS
An imprint of Simon & Schuster Children's Publishing Division
1230 Avenue of the Americas, New York, New York 10020

For information about special discounts for bulk purchases,
please contact Simon & Schuster Special Sales at 1-866-506-1949 or business@simonandschuster.com.
The Simon & Schuster Speakers Bureau can bring authors to your live event.
For more information or to book an event, contact the Simon & Schuster Speakers Bureau
at 1-866-248-3049 or visit our website at www.simonspeakers.com.
Book design by Laurent Linn
The text for this book was set in Aldine 401 BT Std.
The illustrations for this book were rendered in two and six B pencils and acetone markers.
Manufactured in China
0717 SCP
First Edition
2 4 6 8 10 9 7 5 3 1
CIP data for this book is available from the Library of Congress.
ISBN 9781481442275
ISBN 9781481442299 (eBook)

A NOTE ABOUT THIS STORY

This is a very personal story and dear to my heart. It is about a very special little dog that I came to know many years ago. The first time I saw her was back in 1962, shortly after I had graduated from high school. One of my relatives was stationed on the US Coast Guard base at what was then Government Island, on the western tip of Alameda in the San Francisco Bay. I lived in nearby Oakland, and he had offered to take me on a tour of the base.

We were walking near one of the barracks when I spied an ancient little yellow dog. It was apparent that she had given birth to so many litters of pups that her once-muscular little body was now round and sagging in the middle. But when I heard her story and how she came to be there at the base, I was convinced what an amazing dog she was.

Patricia Polacco

"What will the Ol' Man say?" one of the guys piped up.

"Davie, if the Ol' Man catches her in here, he'll order her to be taken to the pound, and you know what will happen to her there!" another said.

"Well . . . I'm a-keepin' her!" Davie Bunch said defiantly. "We're just gonna have to hide her and keep her hidden from the commander!" he insisted.

So from that day on, all of them agreed to keep her hidden on the base!

Davie named her Vera, after one of his favorite aunts. Sure enough, just about all the guys in his barracks fell hard for that little dog! Pretty soon she was standing watches with them. She'd march the quad and do drills with them. She stood at attention during morning reveille and even went out on the bay aboard the buoy tenders.

Just as sure as there are waves in the sea, Vera became a constant fixture in the barracks. All the boys loved playing with her, but most especially Davie. He even taught her to do amazing tricks!

"Watch this, fellas . . . she can fetch anything!" Davie crowed.

Then he'd throw her a toy. Nothing was too far, or too high, or too difficult for Vera! She could run the fastest, jump the highest, and even swim the hardest just to retrieve her toy.

One blustery day a distress call came into the squawk box.

"Mayday! Mayday! We're crashed on the rocks . . . we're sinkin' fast!" an urgent voice rang out. "We're a mile off the Farallones National Marine Sanctuary," the voice went on.

Davie and his company mustered and raced to the dock and boarded one of the search-and-rescue cutters. Vera was right behind them.

That day the Ol' Man happened to be aboard, pulling a surprise inspection.

"Cast off, mates—lives hang in the balance!" he bellowed.

With that the cutter raced across the bay and out under the Golden Gate Bridge, and then took a heading due west, bound for the Farallones National Marine Sanctuary.

Just at that moment a terrible squall came up, and the seas were high and choppy!

When they finally got to the disabled boat, it was listing to port and taking on water fast! The folks aboard looked scared out of their wits. "Hurry up, men—those folks need rescuing. Put on lively steps now!" the Ol' Man boomed. The trouble was that the rough seas, the fierce winds, and the rip currents made it impossible for the cutter to come alongside the sinking boat.

"We'll have to bust them a line. Then we'll rig a bosun's chair and pull them off that vessel onto the cutter!" the Ol' Man roared.

But when they aimed the line cannon at the deck of the stricken sailboat and fired it . . . it missed!

Again and again, time after time, it missed the deck. The winds were just too strong! It was exactly at that moment that Vera appeared at the Ol' Man's feet and started barking.

"What in the name of Billy's barnacles is this?" he hollered as he glared at Vera.

ryone on the crew stiffened and looked at Davie. He saluted and quickly spoke.

here little dog is how we are gonna get a lifeline to those folks, sir," Davie piped
The Ol' Man glared at them both. "This here little dog can jump the farthest I ever
, and she's a strong swimmer." The Ol' Man snorted. "She's already in a vest, and we
throw a line to her and she'll deliver it right to them," Davie said as he pointed at the
king boat. The Ol' Man glowered at Davie and Vera. "Them folks are running out of
, sir," Davie pleaded.

he Ol' Man gave another snort. "All right . . . all right . . . we'll give it a try!" he
bled.

avie threw a line to Vera and gave her the sign, and Vera leaped into the churning
s! Davie's heart pounded with fear.

Vera paddled with fierce determination toward the wrecked sailboat. It wa
if she knew that she was the last hope that those people had! Everyone, includ
the Ol' Man, was cheering her on. Time after time the waves would hide Vera
a trough. She'd disappear only to surface again, paddling ever nearer the distresse
boat. Suddenly she vanished beneath the waves. Everyone fell silent. All that coul
be heard was the howling of the wind.

Vera paddled with fierce determination toward the wrecked sailboat. It was as if she knew that she was the last hope that those people had! Everyone, including the Ol' Man, was cheering her on. Time after time the waves would hide Vera in a trough. She'd disappear only to surface again, paddling ever nearer the distressed boat. Suddenly she vanished beneath the waves. Everyone fell silent. All that could be heard was the howling of the wind.

Everyone on the crew stiffened and looked at Davie. He saluted and quickly spoke. "This here little dog is how we are gonna get a lifeline to those folks, sir," Davie piped up. The Ol' Man glared at them both. "This here little dog can jump the farthest I ever seen, and she's a strong swimmer." The Ol' Man snorted. "She's already in a vest, and we can throw a line to her and she'll deliver it right to them," Davie said as he pointed at the sinking boat. The Ol' Man glowered at Davie and Vera. "Them folks are running out of time, sir," Davie pleaded.

The Ol' Man gave another snort. "All right . . . all right . . . we'll give it a try!" he grumbled.

Davie threw a line to Vera and gave her the sign, and Vera leaped into the churning waters! Davie's heart pounded with fear.

"There she is . . . there she is . . . she's aboard!" Davie cried out. A collective cheer went up that probably could have been heard all the way back to San Francisco! Sure enough, she had ridden a wave right onto the deck! The line was quickly tied to their mainmast, and the cutter sent over a bosun's chair with two frogmen. One by one the wayward sailors were brought to the safety of the cutter. Vera was the last to come aboard. Just as she did, the sailboat sank before their eyes.

"Well, aren't you some kind of hero!" the Ol' Man cooed as he wrapped that wet pooch in a nice warm blanket. From that day on he, too, was in love with Vera. She started spending a lot of time in his office and passed sunny afternoons on a special pillow on his desk. Pretty soon the two of them were inseparable. The Ol' Man even made her the official mascot of the base!

Yes, sir, she'd follow him every day to the mess hall. He even took her on family vacations!

She was his guest of honor at the Admiral's Ball on Treasure Island! She was almost a permanent fixture on rescue missions. She and the Ol' Man had newspaper articles written about them and were even on TV.

By golly . . . that little Vera was putting the Coast Guard on the map!

But what really made her a household name were her courageous actions the day the Sausalito ferry capsized in the middle of the bay.

That morning the ferry was loaded with commuters and their cars. They had just left the jetty in San Rafael. It would never be known why the ferry capsized, but it got caught in the terrible rip currents and was being pulled toward the treacherous shoals off Alcatraz! Rescue cutters and fireboats were dispatched immediately. They got lines to the ferry right away, but there was a small group of passengers still trapped belowdecks. The hatch door had jammed!

The Coast Guard cutter that Vera was on was the nearest to the ferry, and Vera jumped in without a life vest. The waters were freezing, and the Ol' Man feared that the shock of it might drown Vera. But she was undaunted and scrambled aboard the ferry and pulled the tangled pile of rope that was blocking the hatch. She got it open and then stood and barked and barked and barked. All the trapped people followed the sound of her barking to the open hatch door. Every single one of them got out safe and sound. Suddenly the ferry shifted. The hatch door slammed shut and trapped Vera!

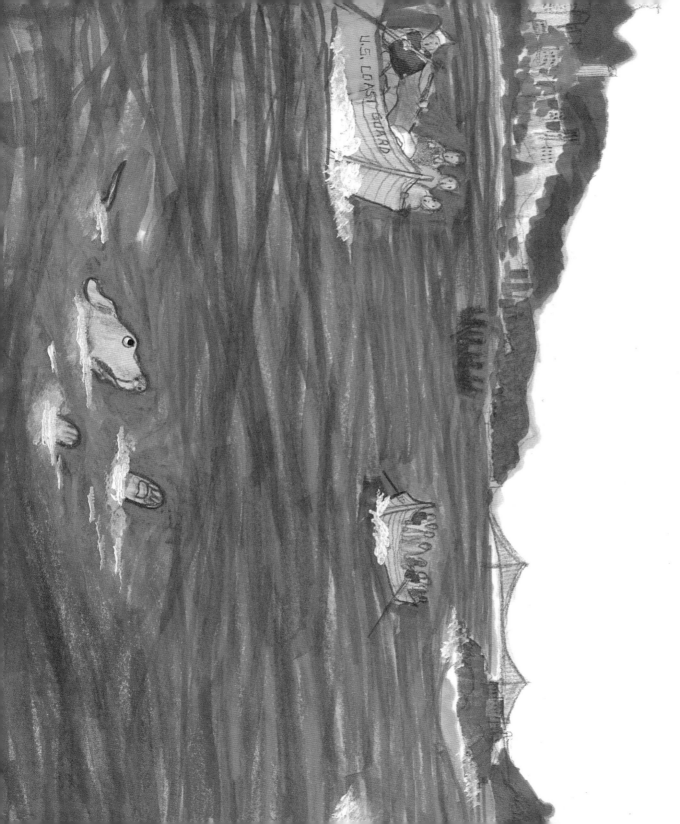

The Ol' Man and his crew just stood there in horror as they watched the ferry disappear beneath the turbulent waters. There was no sign of Vera!

"Vera! Vera girl!" the Ol' Man cried out. But she was nowhere to be seen. The Ol' Man buried his face in his hands and began to openly weep.

"Wait . . . wait! LOOK . . . LOOK!" Davie called.

There she was. She bobbed to the surface. She was too weak to swim and was half frozen and gulping water. Several crew members dove in to get her. When they hoisted her aboard, the Ol' Man couldn't stop hugging her . . . and she couldn't stop licking his face!

From that day on the Ol' Man saw to it that Vera got a nice thick steak every day! Needless to say she received the finest veterinary care as well. But even with all the pampering, her recovery was long. There was residual damage to the muscles of her hind legs, probably from being in the frigid water too long. Finally the Ol' Man made sure that Vera received a medal for valor, and he made her an honorary member of the US Coast Guard. The ceremony was held right on the quad, just under her favorite tree. Then Vera was officially retired from active duty. But she remained on the base for the rest of her days. Twice a year Vera gave birth to a litter of puppies. All of them found wonderful homes. Everyone wanted a part of brave little Vera!

In the spring of 1967 I was working at the Oakland SPCA. One day a young coast-guardsman came to the door carrying a very old dog covered by a blanket. He placed it in front of me on the counter. "She's very old . . . blind and deaf, too. . . . But now she can't even eat . . . nothing stays down," he said sadly. "I'm here on orders to have her put to sleep," he added.

I knew who was under the blanket. I pulled back a corner and it was Vera! I personally carried her down the hall to Dr. Canner's surgery. He had been treating Vera all these years. We both sighed. I held her in my arms as she peacefully and gently drifted into her well-earned rest. When I got back to the reception room, the young man was gone. Probably overcome with emotion. So I called the Coast Guard base to see what they wanted done with Vera. I was told that they would call me in a few hours.

It wasn't more than an hour later that the door to the SPCA waiting room flung open. A complete military honor guard marched in! There was a commander, two staff bearers, four pallbearers, and, behind them, two coastguardsmen in full dress carrying shiny rifles in full salute. All the office staff were asked to stand at attention in honor of a fallen hero. Then we all processed silently behind the honor guard to the surgery, where Dr. Canner and I had laid Vera in state. They placed her in the coffin, then draped it with the American flag. They all saluted. They requested that we escort them to the waiting van at the front of the building.

Every person we passed was struck silent. Men dragged their hats off their heads. Women put their hands across their hearts. Children bowed their heads . . . some of them even saluted. There wasn't a dry eye. Everyone there honored that wonderful little dog!

As I watched the van pull away, I was struck by the thought that somehow my life was meant to intersect with Vera's. I felt honored that I had met her back in 1962 and learned so much about her. How fortunate that I happened to be at the SPCA and witnessed this amazing tribute to her.